Wizziwig
and the
Sweet Machine

for Becky James
G.McC.

for Vanessa
W.S.

ORCHARD BOOKS
96 Leonard Street, London EC2A 4RH
Orchard Books Australia
14 Mars Road, Lane Cove NSW 2066
First published in Great Britain 1995
First paperback publication 1996
Text © Geraldine McCaughrean 1995
Illustrations © Wendy Smith 1995
The right of Geraldine McCaughrean to be identified
as the Author and Wendy Smith as the Illustrator
of this Work has been asserted by them
in accordance with the Copyright, Designs
and Patents Act, 1988.
A CIP catalogue record for this book is available
from the British Library.
1 85213 990 0 (hardback)
1 86039 038 2 (paperback)
Printed in Great Britain.

Wizziwig
and the
Sweet Machine

Geraldine McCaughrean

Illustrated by Wendy Smith

ORCHARD BOOKS

WIZZIWIG'S SHED

Meet Wizziwig, the greatest inventor the world has ever known.

Well, actually, the world does not know about Wizziwig yet.

But one day she will be famous.
She invents things to make the
world a better place.

Together we test her new inventions.

One day I expect we will both be rich and famous.

Not today, but soon.

So on my birthday, she gives me the most amazing presents.

This year was the best of all. When
Wizziwig pulled back the covers,

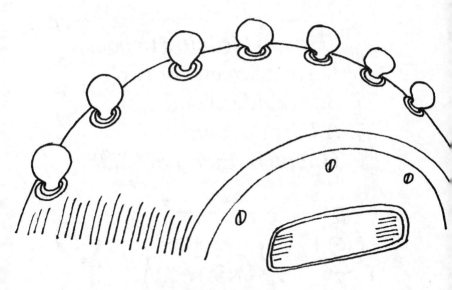

a row of bright lights blinked at
me, red and green and yellow.

Wizziwig took off her hat and sang,

"Happy birthday to you.
Have a sweetie or two.
Suck and savour
All the flavours –
Happy birthday to you!"

"A sweet machine, Wizzi? Do you mean it makes sweets? I have only to press a button and out come sweets?"

"Quite right. What is more, my sweets have no sugar in them, so they are not bad for your teeth."

For a moment I was worried.

I pressed the button marked
FLAVOURS.

The machine rocked on its five feet and sang.

"Hallo,
What do you like most?
Honey on hot toast?
Coffee creams, jellies,
Mangoes or cherries,
Marshmallows,
raspberries,
Nuts, fudge or
strawberries?
Think of the taste
that you like best:
I, your sweet machine ,
will do the rest."

But Wizziwig had gone back to
her shed, to invent something
else.

So I wheeled my machine to school,
to the middle of the playground.

I was the envy of all my friends,
when I told them what it was.

"Show us! Show us!" they cried.
So I pressed the button, lifted the
phone,

and asked for strawberry creams
and sherbet dabs.

I got sherbet creams and
strawberry dabs but they were
delicious.

My friend Sonia asked for jellies

and humbugs.

She got holly and jam cakes,
but they were delicious, too—

even the holly, which was
covered in chocolate.

Then all my friends chose their favourite sweets.

They filled their pockets till they spilled, and crammed their hands.

Boiled sweets
and humbugs
lay all around
on the ground,
like acorns
under an oak tree.

We all had our favourites ...
and then I invented some more–

like mustard marshmallows

and coffee-flavoured crisps,

tomato drops

and walnut chews.

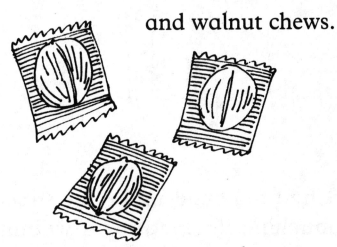

They were utterly, utterly …

DISGUSTING.

"Look out!" said Sonia,
but I did not hear.

I had my head inside the sweet
machine, looking for a walnut
which was clanking about.

I did not see my friends scatter
and run.

I did not see, as they did, that
the Bad-Hat Gang was coming.

The Bad-Hats kicked my
machine with their big boots.

So I asked the machine,

"Double double, make some bubbles,
Make some gum and make it quick.

If you don't, then I'm in trouble,
So make it big and make it stick!"

The sweet machine rocked on its five feet. Then it began to blow the biggest bubbles you ever saw.

They floated, like soap bubbles,
making rainbows in the sunshine,
just above our heads.

The Bad-Hats stared for a
moment in amazement.
Then they reached up their
hands and grabbed.

And there they stuck.
More bubbles stuck to their hair
and to their boots.

They floated
into the air,
and away
over the school,
catching
the sunlight,
making rainbows,
and a LOT of noise.

I was still watching them go,
when along came Mr Ketchit.

He poked at the buttons with his
long, thin fingers.

My machine twirled on its
castors,

and I saw a word flashing at the
back:

The sweet machine had run out
of ingredients.

But Mr Ketchit did not care.
He began to push my machine
towards the school gate, pushing
with all his might.

I think he must have slipped on
the boiled sweets and humbugs.

I'm sure my machine did not eat
him on purpose.

But suddenly Mr Ketchit was
gone,
and the machine no longer said:
EMPTY – EMPTY – EMPTY.

Oh dear! The sweets after that tasted very odd indeed.

The butterscotch was rancid.

The cream eggs were addled.

 All my sweets were sour!

I should never have told the head. She just banged on my machine with a hammer, calling, "Mr Ketchit! Come out of there at once!"

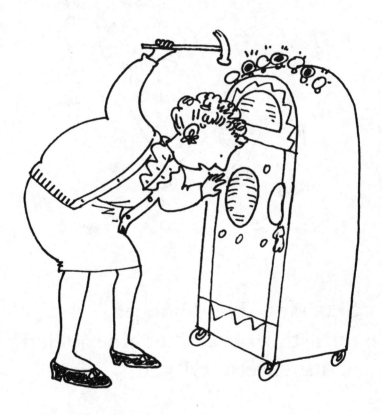

She banged and banged
until the sweet machine reeled
on its wheels and said,

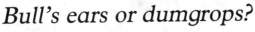

"Goodbye and what's next?
I'm a little perplexed:
Prune juice or snowshoes?
Toadstools or yak-chews?
Bull's ears or dumgrops?
Lilies or jollypops?
Cattle cake?
Rattlesnake?
Nougat from Camembert
cheese?
I am only trying to please."

Suddenly, gobstoppers began to bounce as high as the school chimney.

Chocolate drops exploded when they hit the ground.

Liquorice sticks burned like
sparklers ...

Jelly beans grew into giant
jelly beanstalks.

And the jelly babies cried so loud
we were all sent home early.
It was a wonderful birthday!

But Wizziwig took back my sweet machine to mend it.

She borrowed a piece for her rocket,

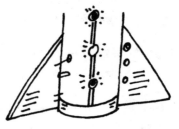

and another for her submarine.

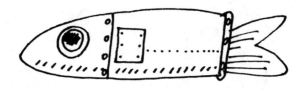

She used the knobs for her robot

and the wires for her radio
(though she sent Mr Ketchit
back to the school).

Soon there was nothing left of my birthday present but its five legs.

I don't mind. It was fun while it lasted. And the school has been much better since the Bad-Hats have been gone.

Here are some pages from Wizziwig's notebook.

What's brown, woolly, covered in chocolate and goes round the sun?
A Mars Baaaaa!

Knock, knock.
Who's there?
Doughnut.
Doughnut who?
Doughnut let anyone else in but me!

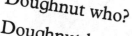

What did the chocolate bar say to the lollipop?
Hi there, sucker!

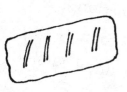

What do you call a clever sweet?
A smartie!

What did the biscuit say to the cookie?
Oh, crumbs!

The largest
sweet ever was
a marzipan chocolate,
made in the Netherlands.
It weighed 1.85 tonnes,
the same as three small cars!

What do climbers eat for dessert?
Rock cakes!

The world's largest ice lolly weighed 5.6 tonnes and was made in the Netherlands in 1992. That is the same weight as an African bush elephant!

Did you hear about the man who ate a sofa and two chairs?
He had a suite tooth!

Here are some other Orchard books you
might like to read...

A BIRTHDAY FOR BLUEBELL
1 85213 455 0 (hb) 1 85213 456 9 (pb)

TINY TIM
1 85213 453 4 (hb) 1 85213 454 2 (pb)

TOO MANY BABIES
1 85213 451 8 (hb) 1 85213 452 6 (pb)

HOT DOG HARRIS
1 85213 457 7 (hb) 1 85213 458 5 (pb)

BEETLE AND BUG AND THEIR MAGIC RUG
1 85213 729 0 (hb) 1 85213 804 1 (pb)

BEETLE AND BUG GO TO TOWN
1 85213 840 8 (hb) 1 85213 879 3 (pb)

BEETLE AND BUG AT CROAK CASTLE
1 85213 889 0 (hb) 1 86039 008 0 (pb)

BEETLE AND BUG AND THE PHARAOH'S TOMB
1 85213 890 4 (hb) 1 86039 016 1 (pb)